Happy Birthday

In Honor of
Your 60th Birthday,
July 19th, 2004

With Love,
From Your Family,
Tammy, Ed, Mike & Michelle

To Linda, Brian and Sarah Robinson,
and to Gordon Bult, who is always in charge

Text and illustrations copyright © 2003 by Jill Newton

Published by Bloomsbury, New York and London
Distributed to the trade by Holtzbrinck Publishers
Library of Congress Cataloging-in-Publication Data
Newton, Jill, 1965-
Gordon in Charge / by Jill Newton
p. cm.
Summary: Gordon the Goat is in charge of the farmyard until Gordon the Goose arrives to challenge him,
and after a series of competitions gets them in trouble, they learn who is the real boss.
ISBN 1-58234-823-5 (alk. paper)
[1. Bossiness--Fiction. 2. Goats--Fiction. 3. Geese--Fiction.
4. Domestic animals--Fiction. 5. Humorous stories.]
PZ7.N48674 Go 2003
[E]--dc21
2002028338

First U.S. Edition
Printed in Hong Kong
1 3 5 7 9 10 8 6 4 2

Bloomsbury USA Children's Books
175 Fifth Avenue
New York, New York 10010

Gordon in Charge

By Jill Newton

BLOOMSBURY
CHILDREN'S
BOOKS

Gordon was a bossy goat who thought
he was in charge of the farm.

When Gordon gave orders the other
animals obeyed (for a quiet life).

"Heads down, and CHEW! Keep in line, you scruffy bunch of sheep!

You cows! Stop larking about and MOO in tune this time!

One, two, three and LAY those eggs, hens! I want a dozen by lunchtime!"

Then early one morning, a new arrival waddled into the yard.

"Who are you?"
demanded Gordon the goat.

"I am Gordon
the goose,"
said Gordon
the goose.

Gordon the goat blinked. "I really don't think so.
I'm afraid you will have to change your name.
I am Gordon – and I am in charge!"

"No, no, no," laughed the goose. "My name is Gordon. And I'll prove that I'd be much better at keeping this farm in order than you.

"You see the pond behind the barn?" he continued. "If I swim across it faster than you then I am Gordon and I should be in charge."

"I think not," said Gordon the goat. But Gordon the goose was already jumping into the water.

"There you go!" exclaimed the goose.
"I can swim faster, so I'm in charge."
"That's not fair!" bleated the soggy goat.

"You see that gate next to the path?" he asked.
"If I push it over before you that will mean that
I am Gordon and I am in charge."

And hurtling toward the gate with his head down, it took Gordon the goat just one butt to knock it flying...

along with the goose.

"That's not fair!" honked Gordon the goose. "You didn't say 'go.' I have a better idea.

"You see those roses by the house? The one who picks the most can be Gordon **and** in charge."

With a flurry of petals and leaves, both Gordons emerged from the former rosebed with mouthfuls of flowers.

All the other animals were watching by now, enjoying the entertainment and enjoying not being bossed around.

Cow counted up the flowers.
It was a tie.

"Recount!" demanded the Gordons.
So Sheep counted,

then Pig counted, but it was still equal.

"OK," said Gordon the goat.
"This will decide it.

"First one to the top of the barn can be
Gordon. First one to the top is in charge."
"Easy-peasy," honked Gordon the goose.

They climbed and flew and scrabbled and fluttered and both reached the top of the roof ... at the same time.

"I was here first!"

"Who was here first?" they yelled
at the animals down below.

A long,

long way

down

below.

The goat felt wobbly. The goose felt dizzy.
They stopped yelling. Neither of them
knew how to get down. They were
stuck on the roof and felt scared.

"Help!
Help!"

they honked and
bleated together.

A ladder appeared, followed
by a big beardy face.
"Well, well. What on earth are
you two doing?" it said.

"We're Gordon and we're in charge," said the two Gordons.

The big beardy face blinked. "I really don't think so. I am Gordon and I am in charge," said the farmer. And lifting the goose under one arm and the goat under the other, he carried the exhausted animals down the ladder and into the barn.

They had worn each other out.
"I'm very tired," said the goose.
"I'm very tired, too," said the goat.
"Tired of being in charge," they agreed.

They looked at each other, surprised.
Agreeing was easy – and seemed quite a lot safer.

So Gordon the goat and Gordon the goose
agreed that they were happy for Gordon
the farmer to be in charge...

for now...